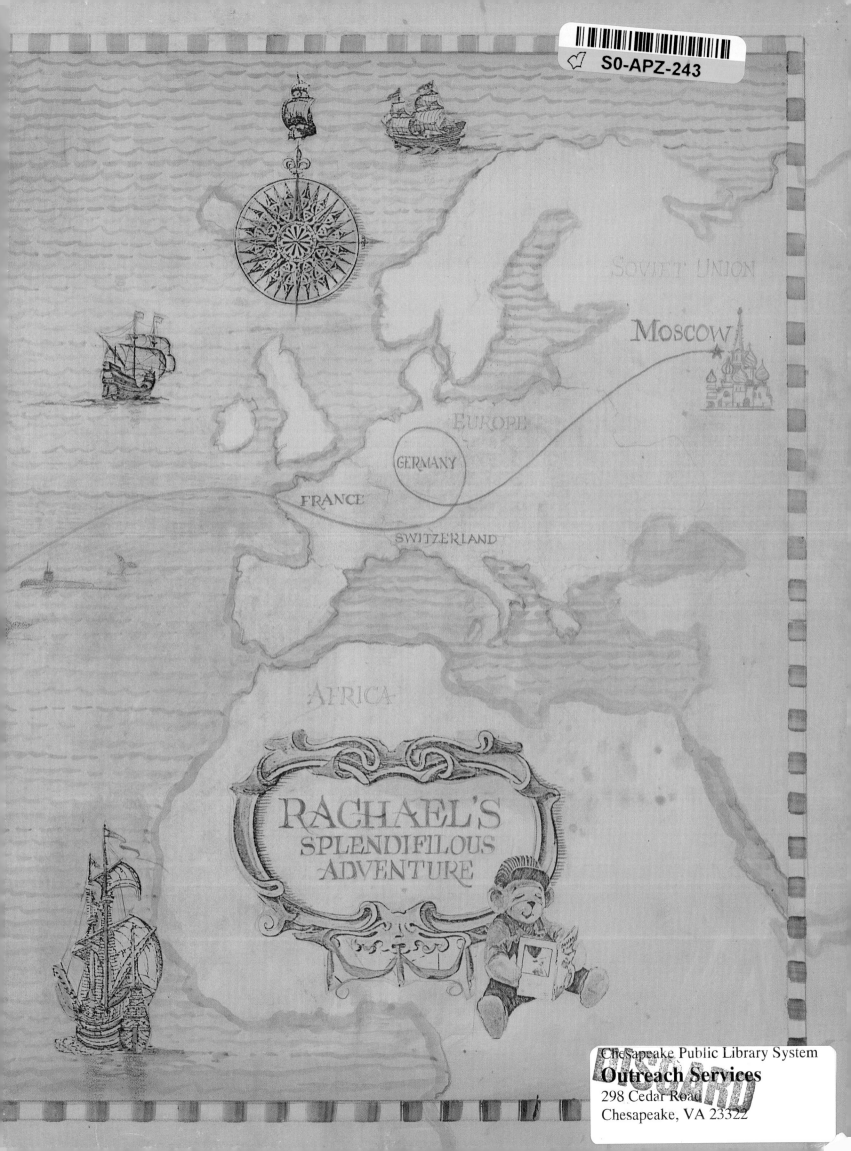

SOVIET UNION

MOSCOW

EUROPE

GERMANY

FRANCE

SWITZERLAND

AFRICA

RACHAEL'S
SPLENDIFILOUS
ADVENTURE

For Rachael and Lauren
and
for Perri, Wendy, and Scott

Thanks to:
Brenda Kildoo
Marilou Tennies

Cataloging in Publication Date
Bansemer, Roger
May, Daryl

Rachael's Splendifilous Adventure

Story of a child's imaginative journey in a hot-air balloon to Moscow. The characters find that people all over the world are more alike than they are different.

Text copyright © 1991 by Daryl May
Illustrations copyright © by Roger Bansemer
All rights reserved
Printed in Hong Kong by South Seas International Press
Second Printing
Library of Congress catalog number 91-066032
ISBN 0-932433-83-9

A WINDSWEPT BOOK
Windswept House Publishers
Mt. Desert, Maine

Other books by Roger Bansemer
<u>**The Art of Hot-Air Ballooning**</u>
(Gollum Press 2352 Alligator Creek Rd.
Clearwater, Fl. 34625)
<u>Southern Shores</u>
(Sentinel Books)

RACHAEL'S SPLENDIFILOUS ADVENTURE

illustrated by
Roger Bansemer
written by
Daryl May
and
Roger Bansemer

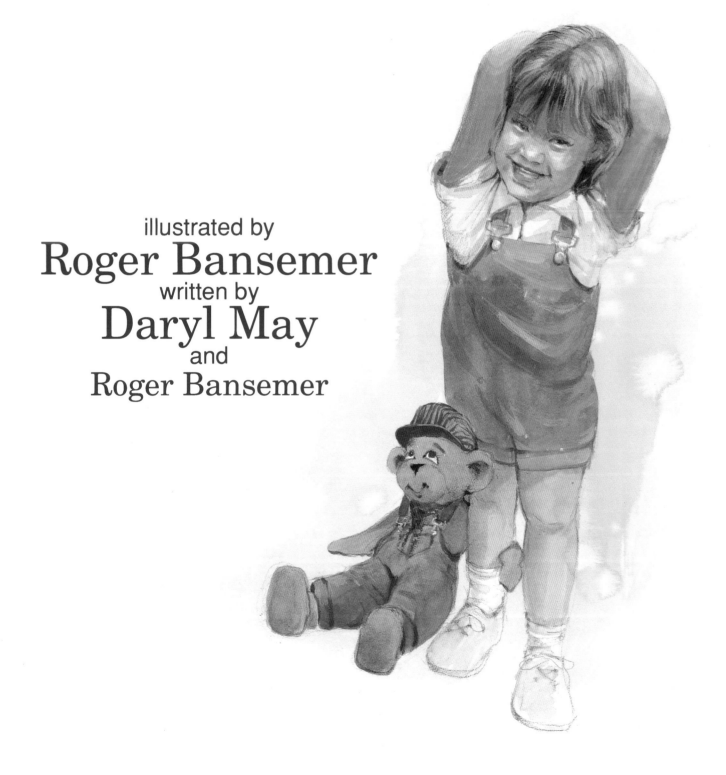

A WINDSWEPT BOOK   Windswept House Publishers, Mt. Desert, Maine

This is a story of a little girl with a big imagination. She had a remarkable adventure that happened in a special dream.

Rachael loved being with her artist father. His studio was in a bright red railroad caboose. Behind the caboose grew a tall oak tree with huge limbs and branches. Hidden behind the high grass and leafy foliage was a cool shallow creek.

During the warm Florida days Rachael played with Captain Sandy, her teddy bear. Her father worked at his easel with his paints. Squirrels ran in the tall grass and played hide-and-seek. Overhead, a white egret flew to a nearby pond.

Nearly every day, Rachael and her dad ate cucumber sandwiches and drank orange juice for lunch. The juice left a bright orange mark on Rachael's upper lip. Then Rachael and her father and Captain Sandy would lie in the hammock for a rest. Rachael and her father would look up to find imaginary shapes in the clouds that drifted slowly overhead.

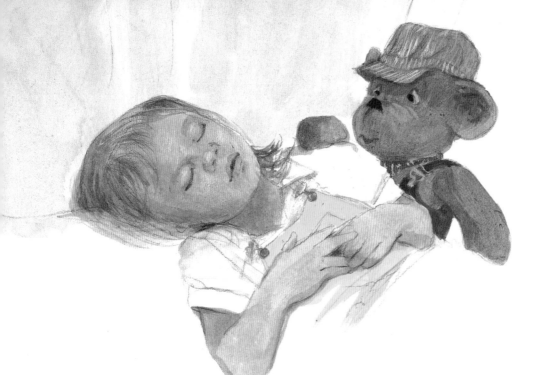

One day Rachael had a dream. In the dream Captain Sandy told her everything about bears. He talked about cub bears, black bears, panda bears, polar bears, koala bears, and even Russian bears. Especially Russian bears!

Then the Captain had what he called a "splendifilous idea." He said, "Let's journey by hot-air balloon to visit my cousin Anatoly. He's a Russian bear who performs with the Russian State Circus in the capital of Moscow."

Just then the giant oak tree over the railroad caboose turned into a bright green balloon. The red caboose became the gondola.

Inside the caboose was a small wood stove. Captain Sandy built a fire. The heat rose through the crooked tin chimney. Soon the balloon filled with hot air.

Captain Sandy said, "Rachael, gather some charts and maps so we don't get lost."

He added, "And you'd better pack a straw basket full of peanut butter muffins, ginger biscuits, and apple crisp on a stick. Mint iced tea for warm days would be nice. Russian hot chocolate, too. It gets cold high above the clouds."

Soon they were ready to lift off. Just as Captain Sandy checked the rope holding the balloon to the ground, Harley, the woodpecker, zipped past the teddy bear's head. "Just where do you think you're going with my house? In case you don't know it, that's my tree you're flying off with." Captain Sandy ducked and bobbed to avoid the angry dive-bombing bird.

"Would...you...PLEASE...relax, Harley! Rachael and I are going on a trip to Russia. Your tree is safe with us. Would you like to come along?"

"Why would you want to go to Russia? If you ask me, you should have your picnic here in America." Harley looked inside the picnic basket. "Besides, I can't eat anything you've packed. Where are the bugs and grubs?"

As the balloon rose gently from the ground, Captain Sandy said, "Come along! I think many surprises await us all."

The balloon looked like a giant Christmas tree ornament as it lifted slowly above the trees. Rachael was sad to leave her father, but he waved and called to her, "Have a good time."

As they soared beyond the clouds, Harley, the downy woodpecker, reluctantly followed close behind. He really had no other choice. His house had turned into a balloon and was leaving without him.

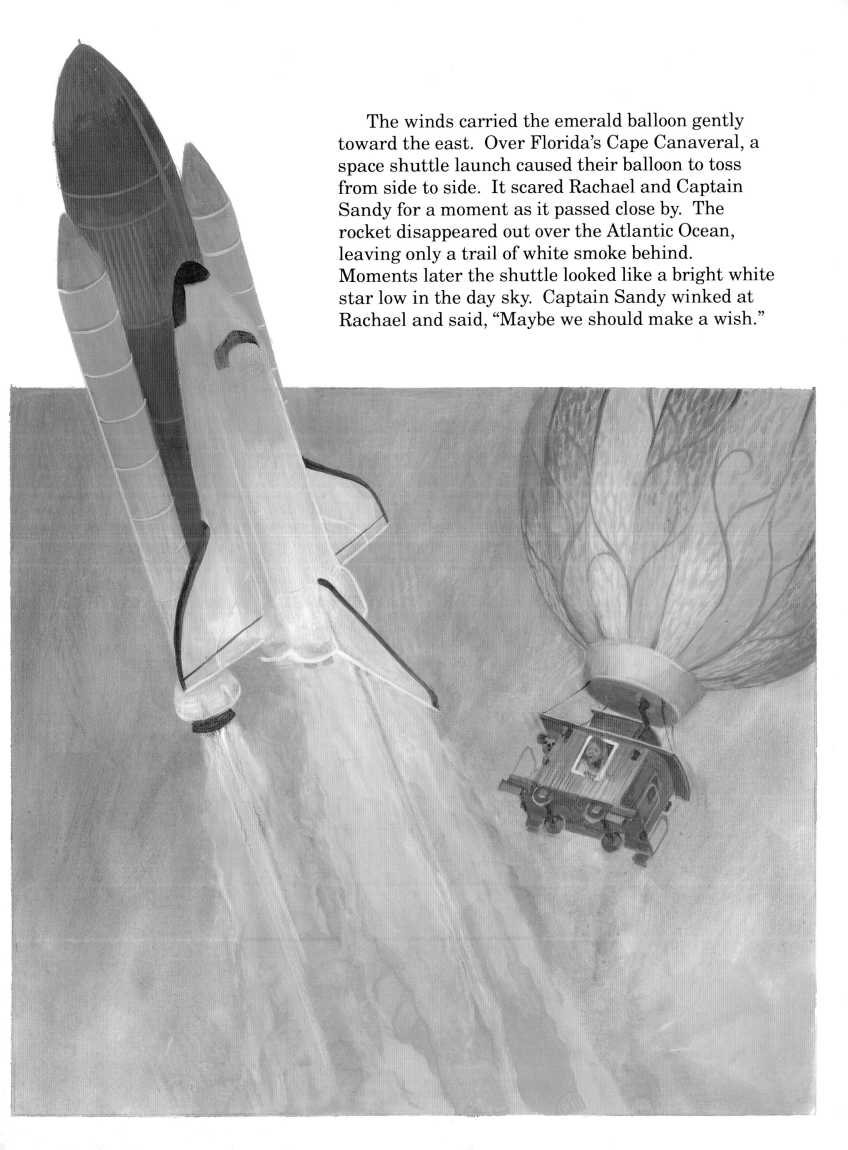

The winds carried the emerald balloon gently toward the east. Over Florida's Cape Canaveral, a space shuttle launch caused their balloon to toss from side to side. It scared Rachael and Captain Sandy for a moment as it passed close by. The rocket disappeared out over the Atlantic Ocean, leaving only a trail of white smoke behind. Moments later the shuttle looked like a bright white star low in the day sky. Captain Sandy winked at Rachael and said, "Maybe we should make a wish."

Hours slipped by, and the little girl and teddy bear continued to sail on their adventure of peace and discovery.

Gentle breezes carried the voyagers beyond the sight of land. All around they could see nothing except the vast blue Atlantic. "It's very cold flying in the clouds," Captain Sandy said, "It's time for hot chocolate, don't you think?"

As Captain Sandy and Rachael sipped from their steaming mugs, a tapping noise came from outside the balloon. "Rachael, did you hear that noise?" Rachael tipped her head for a better listen.

Tap...tap...tap...tap. There it was again. With a trembling voice Rachael whispered, "It's that crazy woodpecker, Captain. He's pecking a hole in the balloon."

"This is serious," bellowed the bear as he scrambled to the roof of the caboose.

"Harley, stop it, right now! You're going to put us down in the middle of the ocean!"

"Don't worry, Cap'n. I'm only eating bugs. I know the difference between bugs and balloons!"

Irritated, the Captain threatened the woodpecker with his slingshot, but Harley continued pecking for food.

"This is your last warning, Harley!" Then Captain Sandy fired a king-sized walnut at the woodpecker. His aim was poor and the nut ricocheted off a branch and punctured the balloon. Hot air hissed out through the hole. Soon the balloon was plunging toward the ocean below.

"Oh, no!" groaned the Captain. "We're in trouble now. We're going down and no one will know what has happened to us!"

"Well, fumble-bear," said Harley, "I can go for help but by the time I get back, you and Rachael will be in the waves."

"It's worth a try," the Captain replied. Harley flew off for help.

Seconds later the wookpecker was back. "Look, Cap'n! Do you see those big dark things swimming below? They're not all whales. There's a Russian submarine down there, too."

Harley zipped back to the submarine and with his beak pecked an S.O.S against the hull. Brap! Bappity...bap...bap! Hatches flew open and Russian sailors raced out. Moments later, the balloon landed on the submarine's deck with a loud thump.

When they saw the damaged balloon, the Russians pitched in to help with repairs.

After the hole had been fixed, good-byes were said, and the little friends once again took to the air. As Rachael waved farewell to the sailors below, she said to Sandy, "What nice people the Russians seem to be. I can hardly wait to land in Moscow!"

The excitement of the unexpected landing on the submarine left Captain Sandy very tired. He crawled into a corner bunk. Soon he was fast asleep. He snored loudly as the green balloon floated steadily toward the coastline of Europe.

From a French village below, a magnificent butterfly air-danced through an open window. It explored the caboose and then, to Rachael's surprise, landed on the tip of Sandy's nose.

Sandy's heavy breathing caused the butterfly's large wings to flutter furiously. The colorful creature hung on for dear life. Rachael found all this very entertaining.

Sandy finished his nap just in time to see a large chateau in the French countryside below. He scurried to the gondola's roof for a better look. It was hard for him to believe anyone actually lived in such a big place. Already knowing the answer, he asked Rachael, "Who do you think lives in such a huge house?" Rachael replied, "People just like you and me, I bet."

Their journey continued over Switzerland's towering peaks, deep snowy valleys, and shadowed gray granite canyons. Harley circled the gondola for a better look.

Sometime later, as the balloon drifted above the green country meadows of Germany, a group of children picnicking near an old wall caught Harley's eye. He decided to investigate.

The woodpecker swooped down and asked the children about the dilapidated wall. The children laughed, danced, and clapped their hands. They called Harley "Herr Woodpecker." They told him the wall had once separated their countries and families. Now the Berlin Wall, as it was called, has been torn down and is no longer guarded by soldiers in high concrete towers. People are now able to visit friends and relatives they have not seen in many years.

Not long after, Rachael and the Captain were gazing down on vast rolling plains. Sandy spoke up, "That's the Ukraine. This region is so fertile it grows most of the food for all of Russia, and Russia is the largest country in the world. It's nearly two and a half times the size of the United States."

The airship gently swept over the thick woodlands. "I'm excited!" whispered the bear. "Can you see the city, Rachael, beyond the forest?" The little girl leaned over the railing for a better look.

"It's Moscow!" sang the Captain. The trees gave way to the dazzling beauty of St. Basil's Cathedral shimmering against the ancient walls of the Kremlin. The church's 400-year-old domes loomed above Red Square.

The giant balloon began its slow descent to the cobblestones. People came running, eager to help with the handling of the ropes. Children giggled at the sight of a little girl and a teddy bear piloting a balloon. And there among the people was Cousin Anatoly, dressed in his circus costume. Under his arm he carried a musical instrument called a balalaika.

After the balloon was safely tethered, Captain Sandy and Cousin Anatoly ran laughing toward each other, arms wide. Like two happy cubs in the wild, they exchanged big bear hugs.

"Anatoly, these are my very dear friends from America," said the Captain. "Let me introduce you to Rachael. And say hello to Harley. He decided to come along at the last minute. We sort of flew away with his tree."

Harley was balanced on Rachael's shoulder. By now, he had decided to make the best of a bad situation. In his best manners, the woodpecker said, "Glad to meet you...I think."

Anatoly took Rachael's hand in his paw and bowed. "I am so pleased to meet both of you."

"Cousin Sandy has told me so much about you," she said.

"Are you ready to see some of the sights?" Anatoly asked. "The people here in Moscow are friendly and warm-hearted. They love this old city and they are proud of it. 'Welcome!' they say to all the world. When you visit Moscow, you're the guests of the Russian people."

Rachael, Captain Sandy and Cousin Anatoly set off hand in hand to explore the Kremlin. Crossing Red Square in the sunlight, they headed toward the main gate. Anatoly pointed out that the walls were 21 feet thick in some places and had taken 10 years to build.

The threesome was followed by the straggling woodpecker. Flitting about in all directions, Harley mumbled that he was hungry.

Within the Kremlin's walls they discovered the Czar Bell, which rests on a platform at the base of Ivan the Great's Bell Tower. "The tower is said to mark the very center of the Kremlin," Anatoly explained.

"The bell sits where it fell and broke after a big fire over two centuries ago. The 200-ton bell, with its 11-ton chip, reflects the grand life-style enjoyed by Russian rulers hundreds of years ago," he added.

"The hole looks like a doorway," said Sandy. "I bet a whole family could live inside that bell."

Farther on, the visitors admired a huge ornate cannon. Called the Czar Cannon, it was built to shoot an iron ball weighing as much as two small cars. "The cannon weighs 38 tons and is 17 feet long. It was made about the same time as the Czar Bell. Like the jumbo bell which never rang, the Czar Cannon was never fired," Anatoly told his listeners.

"Gee," exclaimed Rachael, "just imagine, the cannon and bell have been sitting here since before America had its first birthday!"

They left Harley teetering on the end of the cannon. He stared into the long barrel. "Boy, it sure is dark down there," he uttered.

BOY, IT SURE IS DARK DOWN THERE!

His voice came back at him in a deep echo. Startled, he flew away to join the others. He was glad to get away from the gloomy old gun.

The two bears, the little girl and the
woodpecker came to the Annunciation
Cathedral with its beautiful gold domes.
A flock of crows caught Harley's eye.
They seemed to find it a favorite place to
play. Harley swooped down and asked
Anatoly to tell him about these birds.

Anatoly had many stories to tell about the crows. "In wintertime, they gather on the largest dome of the cathedral. They slide down the icy dome on their feathered backsides, then sail off, like little black bobsleds, into thin air!"

In summertime the crows entertained themselves differently. "Look at that one!" Anatoly bellowed as a prankish bird dropped a pebble down a cathedral rain pipe. The crow then flew to the ground and listened as the stone bounced and banged to the bottom. Anatoly turned and told Harley, "Sometimes the crows spend hours amusing themselves at this caper."

"You really can't expect much more from crows," mumbled Harley.

Spinning on his heels, Anatoly announced, "All right, my friends, the next stop is the circus. Let's hurry. We don't want to be late!"

They hurried on to the circus. Rachael and the Captain took ringside seats. Harley perched on the Captain's shoulder. They sat beside an old lady who looked like Mother Russia herself. Her round face was pink with good health. The wrinkles around her eyes told of her hard but happy life. Her name was Nila.

Suddenly the crowd jumped up cheering. The circus had begun. Anatoly appeared in the spotlight. Behind him were uniformed cossacks who danced to the happy music played by the band. The dancers wore fur hats and shiny black boots that flashed in the lights.

For Anatoly's next act he sat atop an elephant that balanced on its trunk while its hind legs pointed high in the air. The spotlight narrowed on Anatoly as he began to strum the balalaika. "This song is for children everywhere," he called to Rachael. The crowd grew silent when he began to sing.

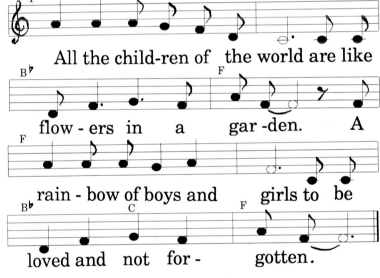

All the child-ren of the world are like flow-ers in a gar-den. A rain-bow of boys and girls to be loved and not for-gotten.

Anatoly's song pleased the audience and gave them something nice to think about.

Suddenly to everyone's surprise, Anatoly invited the Captain to join him in the next act. Sandy was frightened but trusted his cousin. He knew balancing in a chair high above galloping horses would be very different from floating quietly in a balloon. There was a nervous look on Sandy's face. Nevertheless, he joined the excitement and made the high climb to the chair.

The horses galloped around the ring several times. For the grand finale Anatoly tossed the chair and little bear high above his head. Sandy somersaulted in the air and landed gracefully in front of Rachael.

Anatoly's encouragement had helped Sandy perform a most difficult act. The teddy bear's heart pounded with excitement. He took a very low and graceful bow as the crowd cheered his accomplishment.

Nila turned to Rachael and said, "My, those two comrades certainly trust each other."

"Oh, yes!" Rachael said, "Just as Captain Sandy and I have learned to trust each other through all of today's adventures."

"Don't you think Anatoly has shown Sandy something very important?" Rachael asked.

"Yes," replied Nila. "With encouragement Anatoly has shown Sandy he has a talent he was not aware of. We all have talents, but until they are developed they stay hidden within us."

The star-struck Sandy rejoined Nila and Rachael who had become good friends. "You are so pretty, much like my granddaughter," Nila said. Rachael blushed and thanked the kindly old woman.

"And you are an American!" Nila went on. "Even though there are differences in our countries, people are all really the same. We are all the flowers of one garden."

Nila pulled something from her bag. It was a toy with brightly painted flowers on it. She called it a metreshka. Rachael saw it was a hollow wooden doll with other smaller hollow dolls inside, like a beautiful puzzle.

"You see the dolls are different," Nila told Rachael with a gentle smile, "but look at them closely: they are the same...just like all of us."

Rachael thanked Nila for the wonderful gift. They exchanged addresses, writing on the back of Captain Sandy's fancy calling cards. "Now we can write to each other," said Rachael.

As one circus act followed another, Rachael grew drowsy. What a long, exciting day! The close call with the space shuttle, an encounter with the Russian submarine, flying over the Berlin Wall, a tour of the Kremlin, meeting Nila, and now the excitement of the Moscow circus — it had been a very big day.

Rachael's bright eyes grew heavy and her head nodded softly against Nila's shoulder. The little girl fell asleep with the day's events spinning in her head.

"Wake up, Rachael," her father whispered. He gently rocked the hammock. Rachael sat up slowly with a sleepy look in her eyes.

"Would you and the Captain care to join me for a glass of mint iced tea? It's a hot day." Without waiting for an answer, her father walked toward the studio. Over his shoulder he called to Rachael, "And where did the beautiful metreshka come from?"

Rachael pulled the metreshka apart and found a slip of paper with Nila's address written on it. The little girl knew her father would never believe what had happened. "I found the metreshka in a garden...of boys and girls," she whispered to no one in particular. Then Rachael glanced down just in time to catch a sly wink from the Captain's shiny button eyes.

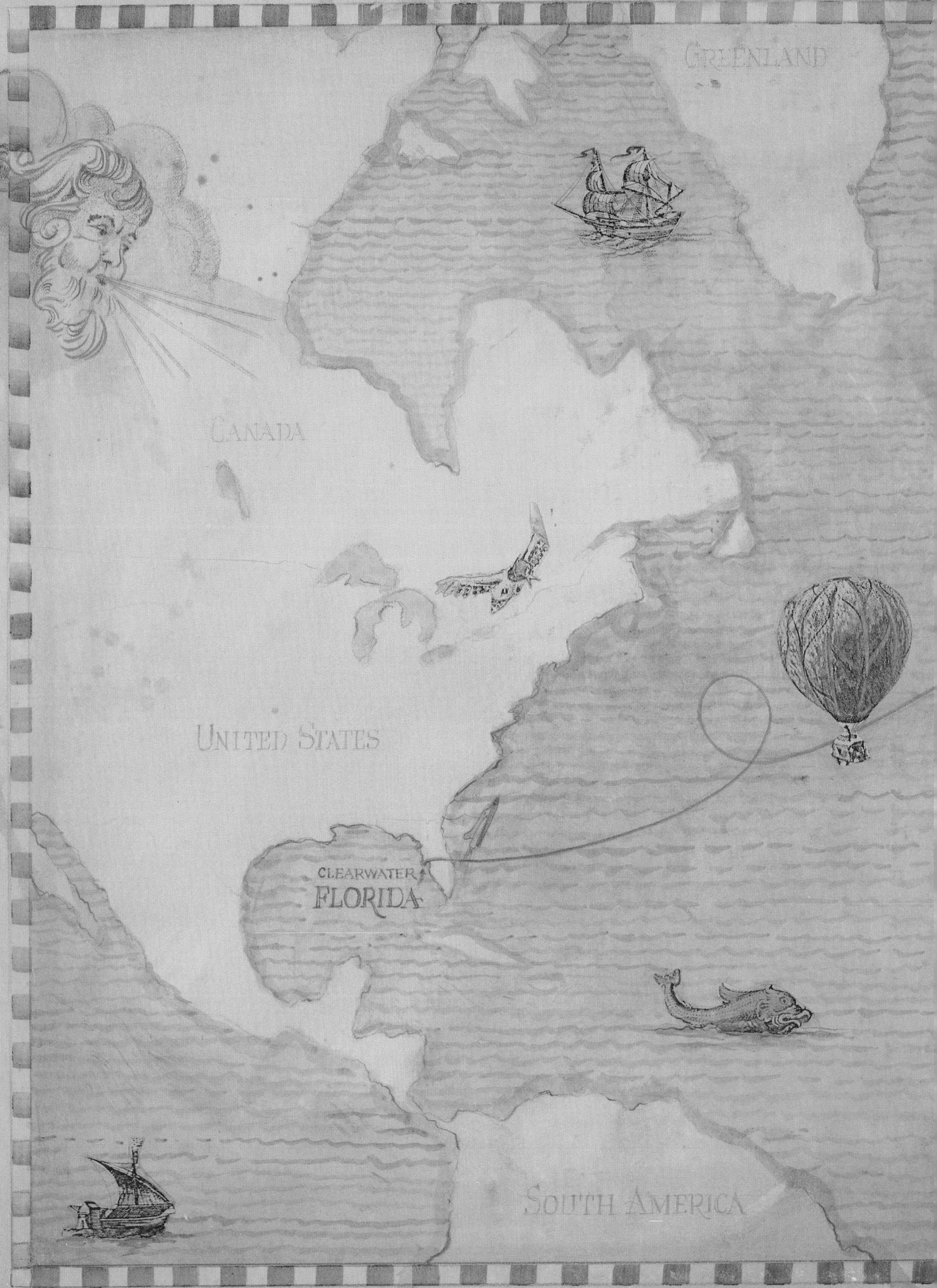
GREENLAND
CANADA
UNITED STATES
CLEARWATER
FLORIDA
SOUTH AMERICA